E   740803
Hal   10.95
Hallinan
For the love of our earth

For the
Love of Our Earth

Written and illustrated by
P.K. Hallinan

For Tim and Munyin

FOREST HOUSE ™
School & Library Edition

740803

FOREST HOUSE ™

This 1992 School and Library Edition published by FOREST HOUSE PUBLISHING COMPANY, INC.

Printed and bound in the United States of America.

Forest House Publishing Co., Inc,
P. O. Box 738
Lake Forest, Illinois 60045

ISBN 1-878363-73-5

Publisher's Cataloging in Publication Data

Hallinan, P. K.
    For the love of our earth / Written and
illustrated by P. K. Hallinan.
                p.   cm.
    SUMMARY: A group of young children show
their love for the earth and their "brothers"
by cleaning up the environment and by not
tolerating prejudice.
    ISBN **1-878363-73-5**
    1. Earth--Fiction 2. Environmental pro-
tection--Fiction. 3. Prejudices--Fiction
4. Stories in rhyme I. T
PZ7.H38F6   [E]   CIP

For the love of our earth,
we'll clean up the land.
We'll pick up the litter.
We'll sift through the sand.

We'll comb every byway,
each sidewalk, and lawn
till everything glows
like the very first dawn.

For the love of our earth,
we'll nurture new trees.
We'll bring back the flowers.

We'll bring back the seas.

We'll clean all the rivers,
the lakes, and the streams
till pure water shimmers
like radiant beams.

We'll stop using engines
that sputter and spark.

We'll stop needless burning
that makes the land dark.

Then taking ahold
of the work to be done,
we'll lighten the sky
and we'll brighten the sun.

For the love of our earth,
we'll try to renew
the bountiful garden
our ancestors knew.

We'll harvest our crops
to help feed the poor.
We'll share what we have,
so that all can have more.

We'll fix up the ghettos,
the shacks, and the slums,
so that each person holds
a safe place in the sun.

And we'll slowly erase
a century of waste.

For the love of our earth,
we'll choose to be kind;
we'll open our hearts
as we open our minds.

**We'll reach out in friendship
to help one another.**

We'll listen with love
to the problems of others.

And never again
will color or creed
be used to determine
who'll follow or lead.

for the love of our earth.